LITTLE KIT
or, The Industrious Flea Circus Girl

EMILY ARNOLD MCCULLY

DIAL BOOKS FOR YOUNG READERS *New York*

London in the mid-nineteenth century was known for material comforts and grinding poverty. Poor children, especially, were cruelly exploited. The city was also famous for novel entertainments—among them, the flea circus.

Fleas were meticulously costumed and harnessed to heavy coaches and other objects, or to each other. When provoked by music or a rap on the stage, they jumped frantically, appearing to perform humanlike feats: moving their burdens about, simulating duels, or making music. The illusion created was that the fleas had been "trained" and so were "industrious." This strange institution persisted well into the twentieth century—as did child labor. But it was street urchins like Little Kit, not fleas, who were industrious. They had to be in order to survive.

E. A. McC.

Published by Dial Books for Young Readers
A Division of Penguin Books USA Inc.
375 Hudson Street · New York, New York 10014
Copyright © 1995 by Emily Arnold McCully
All rights reserved · Designed by Atha Tehon
Printed in Hong Kong
First Edition
1 3 5 7 9 10 8 6 4 2

Library of Congress Cataloging in Publication Data
McCully, Emily Arnold.
Little Kit or, The Industrious Flea Circus girl / Emily Arnold McCully.—1st ed.
p. cm.
Summary: In hopes of a better life, a young orphan girl disguises herself as a boy
and goes to work for the cruel Professor Malefetta and his flea circus.
ISBN 0-8037-1671-0 (trade).—ISBN 0-8037-1674-5 (library)
[1. Orphans—Fiction. 2. England—Fiction. 3. Fleas—Fiction.]
I. Title.   II. Title: Little Kit.   III. Title: Industrious Flea Circus girl.
PZ7.M478415Li 1995 [E]—dc20 93-40658 CIP AC

*The artwork was rendered in watercolor on watercolor paper
with pastel highlights.*

Every day at dawn an orphan waif bought flowers at Covent Garden, tied them in bunches, and sold them in Piccadilly Circus. She did not remember her parents, but was sure they must have loved her. Her name was Little Kit.

An alley near Drury Lane was Kit's home. Here a ragtag group of peddlers shared what little they had.

One evening a man barged into the alley and shouted, "I am the Great and Incomparable Professor Malefetta!" Kit was impressed. "Will I find a good lad here?" the professor went on. "I offer a bed, meals, a few pence for hard work—and the company of artists!"

"Artists?" Kit asked.

"I manage a novelty act," said the professor. "They perform feats you will scarcely believe. The gentry flock to see them."

Kit's heart leapt. Show people! That sounded so far removed from the wretched life of the streets.

"Come, come," said Malefetta. "Will no one speak up? I need a helper who is reliable in every way."

Why, that's me, Kit thought.

"What's your name, lad?" he asked her. Startled, Kit was mute. She wasn't a boy, of course, but she looked like one in her cast-off clothes.

"It's Kit!" blurted Feargus Furze. "Right, Kit's an excellent worker," others said. Kit scanned their faces. They were not going to give her away!

The professor beckoned. No important person had ever even looked at her before. With a last smile for the only family she'd ever known, Kit followed him out of the alley.

They rode to Maiden Lane in the professor's wagon. It was the first time Kit had gone anywhere except on her own two feet.

The professor led her into a small theater with a tiny stage—under a magnifying glass. "Here are the artists," he said. "The one and only Industrious Flea Circus!"

FLEAS! Kit held back tears of terrible disappointment. Fleas were all too common in the alley. But when the professor rapped on the stage, Kit peered at the glass in spite of herself.

The fleas frantically waltzed, fired a cannon, dueled, walked a tightrope, marched, played the instruments of an orchestra, pulled a battleship, and raced coaches. Why, they were amazing, really, Kit thought.

"They do a dozen shows a day," the professor said. "I obtain them from bootblacks and train the ones with talent. Of course, there are tricks to their tricks. I offer illusion to the public." He dropped a heavy hand on her shoulder. "But I will not be fooled myself! Mind you remember that!"

Kit shivered with her secret. Still, if she worked hard, he would never know she wasn't a boy.

Patronized by the Royal Family

SEE
the Amazing
INDUSTRIOUS FLEA

Kit's new life began. She swept, took tickets, scrubbed the glass, and brushed the professor's coat and hat. Her charges jumped for their keep all day long. For their daily feeding the professor matter-of-factly bared his arm. Kit cringed, but there was a little justice in it.

At night the fleas were given to Kit. She put them to sleep in a box among tufts of wool, still chained to the heavy objects that prevented escape. "Poor, exhausted little creatures," she murmured. The sight of their silken chains never failed to touch her. The fleas were prisoners, just like her!

For even as the fleas suffered, so did she. Her bed turned out to be a scrap of blanket on a narrow plank; her meals, bread crusts in the morning and gruel at night. The professor spoke harshly to her when he spoke at all. The pence he had mentioned did not appear. But Mrs. Smudge, the landlady, slipped her an occasional cake and even an orange once.

She didn't object to her tenants; indeed she said, "I think they are the prettiest little merry things in the world. I never saw a dull flea. But watch out for that professor!"

Kit had Mrs. Smudge for comfort, but she wished there was some way she could ease the torment of the fleas.

A stream of people with fine clothes and haughty airs came to marvel at the "learned" fleas who could pull four hundred times their weight. By now Kit knew that the fleas were only jumping—they weren't learned at all, but simply chained to their loads. Secretly she studied the spectators, who could come and go as they pleased, on full stomachs. However miserable life had been in the alley, there Kit had been free!

One day when Malefetta was gone, Speck Slyte, a thief from the neighborhood, came skulking around. Little Kit grabbed the cashbox to safeguard it, and soon Slyte went on his way. When Malefetta suddenly reappeared, he shouted, "What are you doing with my money?"

Kit tried to explain, but he snatched up his stick and landed some blows about her arms and back, crying, "I'll teach you to fool me!" After that she kept an eye on his stick. His terrible temper flared without reason.

Spring came, and even London was balmy. "We're pulling up stakes," the professor announced one evening. "It's time for the Nettlegreen Fair."

"Oh, you'll enjoy it," said Mrs. Smudge. "The countryside is glorious."

Kit ran to whisper the good news to the fleas: Whit, Myrtle, Violet, and the others she had named. Soon she would see meadows and hills and woods and water that ran, not foul in a gutter, but fresh over glistening stones!

They set off for Nettlegreen the next morning. "Smell the air, little friends," Kit said to the fleas. "Each breath is fresher than the last!"

But as they put up the tent, Malefetta warned, "Don't dare stray from this spot, Kit." Then he gave her a long, suspicious look. "You seem different in this light," he remarked. Kit swallowed hard and met his stare.

Between shows Malefetta left Kit in charge and went off to visit his cronies. A girl and her mother came along with a load of cream, eggs, and cheeses to sell.

"They look so good!" Kit exclaimed. "But I haven't any money."

"They're from our farm on the great estate down the road from here," said the girl proudly. "Won't you have a taste anyway?"

Kit was speechless. The cheese was the best thing she had ever eaten.

"My name is Nell Derry," said the girl. "What's yours, lad?"

"Little Kit," she answered. Just then she saw a hand dart toward Mrs. Derry's purse. "STOP, THIEF!" Kit cried.

"Oh, thank you," said Nell's mother as the pickpocket ran off. "All our money was in that purse!"

"I'll see you tomorrow," said Nell with a grateful smile.

The next day Kit watched the passing crowd eagerly. When Nell came, she had more cheese and a sausage for Kit. "This will be good for you," she said. "You look a bit thin."

"I have only my crusts and a bowl of gruel," Kit admitted.

"How dreadful," said Nell. "For supper we sometimes have lovely pudding."

"I'm sure it's delicious," Kit said longingly.

"I'll send my brother Jack around with some tomorrow," Nell said.

"He's awfully nice, and you need a friend. You must be lonely here." She turned to leave.

"Oh, please don't!" Kit blurted, and hastily added, "It's *you* I want for my friend!"

"But I only meant..." said Nell.

"I am a girl too," whispered Kit.

She saw amazement and delight on Nell's face just as Malefetta snarled, "What's this? I don't pay you to loaf about and jolly the maidens!"

He watched her more closely in the days that followed, but shady business deals around the fair still took him away. The moments Kit stole with Nell were the happiest she had ever known.

"We have a school on the estate," she told Kit one morning. "And there are lovely animals…sheep and cows, horses and pigs, chickens, dogs and cats. Mother can't bear to turn away even a stray kitten!" When Kit told her in turn about her old life in London and her new one with the professor, Nell cried, "It isn't fair!"

All day long Kit thought about Nell. She was musing over her friend's words that evening while she bathed. Malefetta had gone to gamble somewhere. There was a sound outside. She met the spiteful eyes of the pickpocket.

"Well, well!" the thief chortled. "There'll be trouble when Malefetta finds out his lad is a lass, won't there? Oh, he hates to be fooled!"

Furious, Kit threw on her clothes. Anger quickly mixed with fear. What a beating she would get if the pickpocket told what she had seen. Of course she would, but when?

"I must escape without delay!" Kit told the fleas. "I'll be all right.... I'll sleep under haystacks....I'll eat berries and nuts." But beyond that, she could not imagine how to live.

"Good-bye, dear, wee friends," she said. The fleas twitched faintly, and she knew she could not abandon them. Didn't they want their freedom too?

Beneath the magnifying glass, she gently unhitched each insect from its load. Then she put the box of fleas under her arm and stole away.

Kit slipped easily through the crowds of fair-goers. Before long she
was on a country road. The sounds of night creatures filled the air.
"Listen," she said to encourage the fleas. "Isn't it strange and wonderful?"
But she was worried. What lay ahead? She could only trudge on.

Then light shone from a window ahead. Dare she knock at the door?
Respectable people would not welcome a ragamuffin—and ragamuffin
she was, on the outside! She had never begged, and would not now. Yet
how the light beckoned! She would ask to sleep in their barn. Shivering,
she knocked.

When the door opened, Kit gave a cry of joy. And so did Nell! "You've run away! Oh, how wonderful!" Nell exclaimed, and introduced Kit to her parents and brother. Kit stood trembling as her friend explained her plight.

Nell's mother and father clucked and shook their heads when they heard about Professor Malefetta. "Terrible, terrible man," they said.

Then Nell's father turned to his wife and smiled. "Well, my dear," he said, "another lost kit to take in, eh?"

"You mean I may stay the night?" asked Kit.

"We mean we are offering you a home," said Nell's mother.

When the happy laughter died down, Nell took Kit's arm. "Come and try on a pretty dress of mine," she said.

Moments later there was a loud knock at the door. "Open up for the sheriff!" Kit heard, followed by Malefetta's shout, "Are you hiding my reliable lad?"

The sheriff...with Malefetta! thought Kit with a sinking heart. Might Nell and her family be arrested—all because of her? She ran to give herself up.

Malefetta stared blankly at her. "Come, come," he growled. "Speak up! Has anyone seen my lad?"

"There is no lad here but my son Jack," said Nell's mother.

Furious, the professor stomped out of the house.

When bedtime came, Kit showed her box to Mr. Derry.

"You brought WHAT?" he exclaimed. "Oh, well, I guess it can't be helped. They'll have plenty to eat in the barn."

Kit was blissfully happy at the farm and a great help to her new family, who loved her devotedly. In the barn the fleas made the most of their freedom. They became fat and contented, and were never Industrious again.